Mokusei!

Mokusei!

A Love Story

CEES NOOTEBOOM

Translated by Adrienne Dixon

LONDON NEW YORK CALCUTTA

Seagull Books, 2017

Original and translation © Cees Nooteboom, 1982, 1985

First published in English translation
by Bridges Books, Amsterdam, 1985

ISBN   978 0 8574 2 483 9

British Library Cataloguing-in-Publication Data

A catalogue record for this book is available from the British Library.

Typeset by Seagull Books, Calcutta, India

Printed and bound by Maple Press, York, Pennsylvania, USA

For Sjoerd Bakker

1

The photographer, still a young man and in his early thirties, very Dutch in appearance, was walking along a busy shopping street in the Ginza. He was thinking of the photograph he would have liked to take. It was late evening and he felt the chill of the early, northerly autumn. The cool air, perhaps coming from the sea, imparted something rural to the atmosphere, and God knows, maybe this was the reason why he succeeded in not letting the barbarity of his surroundings affect him and thus retained the vision of the woman he would have liked to photograph. His name was Arnold Pessers and he was in Japan for the fifth time. And it was the last, he knew. He also knew that if he were to pay attention to what was around him, he would be filled with hate, a hate he would not have considered possible on his first visit. Japan, he thought, had taken Japan away from him. The two Japans, in which the Japanese themselves moved about so apparently noiselessly and unperturbedly—until someone like Mishima broke the fiction with a flagrant, reckless suicide—had also split him in two, into banalities such as love and hate. This country, these two countries, would never be his. That in itself did not matter so much, but it had also turned against him, with the shattering force of a luckless love affair, so that even his own love had changed into hate. The first time he had said something to this effect, to his friend De Goede, who had been attached to the Cultural Section at the Belgian Embassy for four years, De Goede had laughed in his face. That had been at the time of his first doubts, as long ago as that.

'There are not two Japans, certainly not to the Japanese. To them it is indivisible, if they think about it at all. You have come here, like everyone else, on false pretences. I have seen it all too often. They've read a book by Tanizaki, or maybe they've seen *Shogun*, a Hiroshige exhibition, they've picked up a few half-baked ideas about Zen, and they think they know all about it. It is one big misunderstanding—literally, a misunderstanding. I can always pick them out at once, I only have to have lunch with them. You can't say they are boasting exactly, but they always want you to know that they know the score, that they are old hands, even before they've ever set foot in the place. *Sashimi, suimono, mizutaki*—the words come tripping out of their mouths as if they had never eaten anything else, they practised in Amsterdam at the Okura or at Kyo's, it wouldn't surprise me. Usually they are also very happy here, the first time, provided you organize things properly for them. They want aesthetics, so all Hondas have to be made invisible. They refuse to see the vulgarity, which is what three-quarters of life consists of, here as much as anywhere else, and that is what you have to help them with. So, not too long in Tokyo, but right away to Nikko or by bullet train—oh yes, they want that all right—to Kyoto, no messing around. They insist on sleeping in genuine ryokan, on sitting in a wooden tub with a whole family, they spend long hours in the Kabuki-za and pretend they understand it, visit a monastery if at all possible, where they then find confirmation of their notions about the spirituality of Japan. What they are looking for is a Netherlands where everyone knows Lanceloet by heart, or a Flanders that consisted of nothing but Memlinc, the city centre of Bruges and the finer points of Ruusbroec. Such countries exist only in time, they haven't existed in space for goodness knows how long.'

Arnold Pessers remembered exactly when this conversation had taken place or, rather, he remembered the day, though not the year. The emperor's birthday had apparently been of such mystical significance that the number of the year in which it occurred hardly mattered. He could see it again now. They were standing together in a long line of Japanese, in front of the superhumanly tall gates of the Imperial Palace. The divine presence, so it was said, had already manifested itself in a window two times that day, and it was not certain whether it would appear again. Officers with swords continually straightened the line. Peering past the blades of their swords as though an enemy were approaching on the horizon, they drew an imaginary rope alongside the crowd; any protruding elbow would be hacked off. Arnold Pessers thought of a photograph he had once seen, of a Japanese soldier about to behead a captured Australian pilot who was sitting on a block of wood. He remembered the touching white knees of the blindfolded man, and the raised sword, flashing in the tropical sun, which would swish down in less than a second, whereupon the head would fly through the air and the body, in those ridiculous short pants, would fall sideways. He had often wondered whether he would have taken that photograph, and he thought he would not. He shuddered.

'Doesn't *this* exist in time?' he asked.

De Goede shrugged his shoulders.

'Certainly it does. But what you see is something you assume to be pure, holy tradition. And that is how they like to sell it too. These gates open only once a year. Then the people are allowed just for once to walk on these garden paths that normally only the emperor walks on. And emperors have been here, as you know, ever since the blurred, misty past. Twilight of the emperors! They go back for centuries before Christ. I believe the present one is the 130th. And a direct descendant, too. So you're linked to primeval times here, and that seems to be a happy thought to many people. All I see is a bunch of militaristic bullies who refuse to tolerate the slightest improvisation. This nation is sick with obedience. Don't you dare step out of line.'

Deliberately, De Goede now took a step sideways, thus bending the imaginary rope out of line. Immediately, one of the officers came forward with angry strides, to push him back into place.

'A thousand reproachful eyes now pierce my back,' De Goede said cheerfully, 'But I am a Flemish giant, I can stand it.'

At that moment the immense gates opened.

'What happens now?' asked Arnold.

'Wait and see, and keep your holy visiting card at the ready.'

A slow-moving throng, they entered the imperial gardens or, rather, they were driven like a flock of sheep until they reached, in full view of the massive palace, a row of trestle tables on which all the men, apparently without exception, deposited their visiting cards.

'The Son of Heaven will be reading all these tonight,' said De Goede cheerily. The Japanese around them lingered for a while, gazing at the blind windows, but no one appeared, no man and no god, and with gentle pressure they were led away, to make room for the next group.

Almost mechanically, Arnold Pessers spent a couple of films on the stately, melancholy splendour of the imperial flowers, but his thoughts were still on his friend's earlier words.

'I still don't quite understand what you mean,' he said, after his Leica, with soft sighs and clicks, had swallowed the purple-and-gold magnificence.

'What I mean by what?' asked De Goede.

'By space and time.'

'It's very simple. A manner of speaking. Most of the English and Americans who come here—not necessarily the business-men, for they are undeceived very quickly indeed, but let us say the artistic types— have no real knowledge of Japan at all. They know it's different, but so are Vietnam and the Ivory Coast. Japan, if you will for-give the expression, is differently different. But how do you explain that to them? They don't speak the language and in most cases never will. They know a little, which is really nothing, about Japanese culture, but that doesn't bother them, they have something better than knowledge, they have an *idea* about Japan. And this idea always has to do with a certain form of asceticism or purity or whatever you like to call it. To put it briefly, it comes down to this, that they are convinced that the Japanese have managed better than other people to keep their heritage intact, as if in some kind of pure, unadulterated culture.

'Purity is the watchword. The *pure* beauty of calligraphy. The *pure* aesthetics of flower arranging, of eating, of daily life. The ugliness, the stupidity, the ruthless slavishness with which the Japanese copy our worst habits, the buying of mass products, the ridiculously aped decadence—they refuse to see it. The poetic types are the worst. They never stop talking about the samurai writing poetry at a time when the languages into which these poems are now being translated had not yet been invented. As soon as poets start talking of soldiers and commerce, you'd better watch out. "The samurai class stands by the cradle of the present-day economic miracle in Japan," I read the other day. That was written by a compatriot of yours. Holy mother, they practically believe themselves to be fully fledged Buddhists when they've read a twenty-page pamphlet, they write haikus in their Western hotel rooms, but forget to switch on the television, and they wander around the temple ghetto in Kyoto armed with a *Polyglot Travel Guide* without noticing the differences in style between the various periods. The disappointment always comes later, and then they make a complete about-face. Then they never stop complaining, though without the punch of the true haiku: "The Japanese are so inaccessible, you can't get through to them, they don't understand anything, they don't speak any languages, they just smile politely, they have no individuality, they sell out to the West, they don't deserve their country. And so on."'

'What do you think of Japan then?'

'I think that the Japan they are talking about, the Japan they first talked about, did once exist. Once upon a time. Before we forced it to join us. The madness of it. Wanting to drag by hook or by crook an island that lies like a shrimp stuck against the big belly of Asia into the wake of our morbid progress. Commander Perry. Small events, evil consequences.'

'So there once did exist something like it?'

'Something like it, yes. Perhaps. Once upon a time. Long ago.'

'And nothing is left of it?'

'Enough is. But you have to search for it. And it is not accessible, it never was. To Lafcadio Hearn, perhaps, then. Or to Sieboldt. But not to us, now. We are lazy and they have changed. Although . . . '

'So what do you think of Japan?'

De Goede stood still. For the first time, a shadow of doubt appeared on his usually impassive face.

'I understand nothing about Japan,' he said. 'I know a lot and I understand less and less. Last week they took a German colleague of mine away by Lufthansa, screaming in a straitjacket. "Japanitis" they call it. He spoke Japanese, had done his PhD thesis on Bunraku, he had a Japanese wife, you name it. Ran his head against a wall, exit screaming.'

'East is East and West is West?'

'No, it isn't that,' De Goede said impatiently.

'I spent some time in Bangkok, and in Ulan Bator of all places. No problem. Lots of problems, but no problem. But this mad mixture . . . . There's going to be a big Tokugawa exhibition in London soon, one enormous display of holy, untainted Japan, all of it pure culture. You won't find a hint of the incredible blood-thirsty dictators which the Tokugawas also were. Only their art remains, just as with the Medici. Art can be used for anything, even for selling Toyotas.'

They paused by a group of oddly clipped bushes. They look like animals without heads, thought Arnold Pessers. He did not take a photograph of them. It was as though these bushes were lying on the shorn lawn, as if they could not have roots. He looked at the deep, mournful purple of the maple trees beyond, and then at the people walking towards the exit in silence as if they had experienced something for which no words existed. Suddenly he noticed how much taller and coarser he and his friend looked. A Van der Weyden and a Jan Steen, De Goede had once remarked mockingly, and it was true: in some mysterious way their beloved ancestors had carried those inalienable features, via an infinite progression of matings and pregnancies, unaltered through the ages, into this Japanese garden, and here they stood briefly, more in the role of descendants than anything else, as the solid, pale products of another race. They don't even see us, he thought. They don't want to see us. There was something strange about it, to feel at the same time so solid and yet so invisible, as if you would be able to fly despite your weight. It made him feel slightly dizzy and he decided not to think about it any more.

'And yet I am fond of them,' said De Goede, as if he too had taken stock. 'Do you know what I think is the oddest thing about them? All their greatest heroes are failures. In a country where people prefer to hide in a crowd and not to be noticed, the few madmen who go against the grain and fail hopelessly are the heroes. As long as they fail, as long as their end is cruel and desperate and their doom predictable.

I have a book about it, *The Nobility of Failure*, you ought to read it.'

2

The Nobility of Failure—this title had impressed itself on Arnold Pessers with the force of a slogan, a formula you could mutter softly to yourself and which then acquired a mysterious power. He had remained silent for the rest of that afternoon, but now, so many years later, he recalled the quintessence of that conversation in its full intensity. He entered a fashionable espresso bar and sat down, in the purple neon light that can make the Japanese skin look such a deathly grey. The irritating exemplariness with which the people here were dressed oppressed him, as if he was having an evening out in Zwolle, but he did not want to go back yet to the flat he had just come from. The woman he had left there must be asleep first, only then would he go back. He closed his eyes and saw the photograph he had not taken. 'Après l'amour', it should have been called, he thought maliciously. They had slept together—for the last time in the room where they had slept so often before—two strangers inside a deathly silent cube, human beings, members of a strange animal species that could in no way have anything to do with the ceaseless traffic of the megapolis which, somewhere far below, sounded like a double bass continuously playing the same note. Love making was, with them, usually a soundless event but— he could not think of any other word for it—always dangerous. He had never experienced this with anyone else, this sense of threat, this challenge of anger and warfare coupled with unintelligible professions of love and caresses disguised as bites. But it was exactly for that reason, he knew, that it was love—a love he would have liked to pour over her in buckets, covering that oriental, different, closed body under him, beside him, above him, as with a lasting light, and yet a love that at the same time had always retained a shadow of such terrible intensity that it frightened him, while this fear, in its turn, he did not know how, renewed his love, again and again, rousing and spurring his feelings and his tenderness. He then felt again, humiliatingly, that he was someone of a different race, someone belonging to a cheap, unenduring, banal kind of people that found it necessary to dispel the deeper emotions at all cost, by smoking, telling jokes and anecdotes, small talk, evasion.

So it was this evening. Thinking of the love affairs he had had in his life (the long life of a thirty-four-year-old photographer from Utrecht!) he knew these had never been more than a consumption of each other; two bodies intent on mutual enjoyment. True, this had sometimes been mingled with tenderness, or with that other ingredient which is, usually without justification, called love, but it had never been such a silent, almost vicious fight with the apparent aim of becoming the other, as far as that was possible. Was this nonsense? He was not sure, but it was what he had often thought: that he wanted to become her, and he felt, without either of them ever having said so, that something very similar was taking place in her, that she, mad though it might sound, was trying to take possession of his body, not in order to have him but to *be* him.

He would never be able to explain this to anyone. How can you tell someone, even your best friend, that you can know by the grip of a woman's hand that it is governed by a desire for exceeding any short-term possessiveness, that her hand had grabbed at his bones, his shoulders, his elbows, his knees, his loins, his head, wherever he was more bone than flesh, as if she knew that that was where his essence lay, that his soul resided in the hard, technical parts of his body rather than in the soft ones that would disappear so much sooner. He had learnt to keep such thoughts to himself.

3

He ordered a second espresso. One thing at any rate he was sure of, as he looked at the face of the girl who put his order in front of him, that it was not the Japanese in her that had attracted him in the first place. It was the Japanese *within* the Japanese, he could not express it any more clearly than that. To him, there would always remain something unreal in all those closed faces, but hers had by nature a double layer, not the plastic model of the Westernized doll's head with the clipped eyelids that you saw everywhere around, but a mask underneath the mask, as if an older layer of the population, of the *people* was present inside her. Mongols, Ainus, Kirghiz, a magic, unknown tribe of nomads, a clan from the steppe that had settled within her, so that through her you were connected with long-lost times, with something that no longer existed and that would never come back.

That was how she had looked at him, again this time, when he said he wanted to go out for a short walk. He always had to take care not to lose himself in her gaze for too long, otherwise he would lie sleepless beside her for hours. He had quickly opened the rice-paper sliding door and had stepped out. But before reaching the outer door he had turned around once more. She was already half-undressed and stood in the narrow opening, a white erotic statue, a scarcely moving image against the bare interior of the Japanese room. His vision became double, that of a lover and a photographer. The lover knew he should not have looked back, because she would be lost to him as a result; the photographer, on the other hand, caught the entire image all the more eagerly in a frame: the rice-paper doors, the panels in the narrow wooden surrounds, painted with mountain landscapes in light grey shades, fine, washed brushstrokes hinting at rather than representing nature. Because the door had been slid aside, the landscape no longer matched. It seemed as if even the imagined world had become double, had shifted to one side, while in the centre a void had occurred, behind which, in the middle of the room, she rose like a goddess of doom.

4

The first time he had seen her, five years ago, her face had received the name that he still muttered to himself, whenever he thought of her. *Snowy Mask*. He had come to Japan for an utterly banal purpose: to compile a travel brochure for a distinguished, though of course commercial, organization. But even if it had been a documentary about cement works or prisons, he would still have come. His world, and this was a fact to which he had resigned himself, was the world of brochures, of ephemera that no one would ever look at again; the decay, the sell-out, the morass. It wasn't actually so much a question of having resigned himself to it—he had taken a decision about it. He knew he wasn't good enough to be so independent that he could choose his own subjects, and even if anyone would, it was hardly possible to make a living that way. He had once baffled De Goede, when the subject cropped up, by showing him his favourite photograph.

'I always carry it with me,' he had said, timidly as if it were childish to always carry with you what was dearest to you, like a taxi driver keeping the picture of his wife and children on the dashboard. He had stuck the photograph to the inside of his camera case. It was his talisman, his amulet, but that was nobody's business. It was a page cut from *Zoom*. For a moment it had seemed as though De Goede would burst out laughing. His slightly rotund, soft, white body wrapped in a too-small kimono, had sunk lower into the chair, the hand with the signet ring had held the photograph away from him; he, Arnold, was not allowed to look at it now. But he knew it by heart, as if he had taken it a hundred times. It was a photograph from 1858 and there wasn't really anything in it. He had first seen it in the Notman Photographic Archives, in the McCord Museum in Montreal. His attention had initially been drawn only to the shape, for while the two bottom corners were rectangular, as they should be, the two top corners curved rather oddly so that the whole photograph was shaped like a tunnel, a dark tunnel at that. 'The prairie on the bank of the Red River, Humphrey Lloyd Hime', it said—and this was exactly what the picture showed, a grey, leaden, old-fashioned plain in which prairie and water seemed to merge into each other without distinction. The horizon was a straight line; above it hung an equally desolate sky of a lighter grey, without any nuances. Two fields of grey, in fact, one darker, one lighter. And yet, when you looked longer, something like movement began to appear in those dead expanses of grey, a fraction of the light in the upper area had imparted itself to the darker area below, so that something of the light which had shone on that sombre river that day had been preserved; few streaks, a few patches, a flicker, just as the light of the stars tries to speak of something that happened before there were people and would try to do so even if no people had ever come into existence, although in that case the question arose: Why or, rather, for whose benefit?

In the foreground you finally saw, if you went on looking long enough, a faint, almost dirty line that was supposed to represent the bank, the beginning of the flat, no doubt muddy, land on which the ridiculous photographer must have stood with his tripod, drinking in light in order to record this sad, empty scene without people, trees or animals.

Albumen-silver from a glass negative. It moved him in a way that made him afraid to speak of it, for if he did he would have to say that you really ought to cry when you looked at it.

'*Mono no aware,*' De Goede had said.

'I beg your pardon?'

'"The pathos of things". That is a notion they have here, you'll hear it mentioned plenty of times. It means exactly what it says. It sounds like it, too.'

'*Mono no aware*,' the photographer had repeated the words and had never forgotten them. They fitted the photographer exactly.

'What would you most have liked to photograph, if you didn't have to do all this rubbish?'

'Stones.'

De Goede had laughed, and what was worse, he had been unable to stop, until Arnold Pessers realized that this was meant to indicate a special kind of agreement. But that was all a long time ago.

5

Long ago, and at the same time a sort of yesterday. For that kind of time no verb tenses exist. Memory flows this way and that between the perfect and the imperfect, just as the mind, left to itself, will often prefer chaos to chronology. It was with the passion of a convert—his Flemish friend had not been far wrong in that respect— that he had wanted to go to Japan, as if, so said De Goede, something could still be found there that had vanished almost everywhere else, except perhaps among the Touareg or in the bidden darkness of the

Amazon region, but which at any rate could never be retrieved in the kind of society from which he had sprung and in which he, so it seemed, would have to remain for the rest of his life. The contradiction between these thoughts and the trite travel brochure, for which a lady in kimono against the background of Mount Fuji had been most particularly requested, he had brushed aside, along with the dismal sight of the drab warren of untidy streets, during the endless journey from the overcrowded airport to the hotel that looked exactly like all other hotels, anywhere in the world.

He had refused to feel disappointment and attributed the doubts he was so forcibly repressing to the wretched flight that had lasted for more than twenty hours. If you make up your mind to enjoy yourself you will usually do so. He had invested too much in this visit. He did not switch on the television in his hotel room, but he admiringly examined the manner in which his kimono, put out for him on the bed, had been folded. He also gazed—as if this could banish the rest of the surroundings—at a reproduction of a calligraphic masterpiece, a black, furious trail of unintelligible but beautiful, exciting signs on snow-white paper. He ate in the Japanese restaurant at his hotel, where the food was exorbitantly priced, and delighted in the graceful movements and the high, gurgling voices of the waitresses. That there was something mechanical about these movements, because of the tiny, always identical, shuffling steps with which they went about their business, he did not want to see. He was in Japan. And that he was not going to have taken away from him.

6

The next day he had phoned De Goede, his
friend at the embassy whom he had first
met when making a documentary about
Vietnamese refugees in northern Thailand.
De Goede had made himself available and
together they had gone to a modelling
agency where they worked their way
through stacks of photographs of Japanese
girls. Arnold Pessers had learnt how to
see through the insipidness of such photographs—which were after all merely
intended to sell a living person—but this
time he was unable to find what he was

looking for. The faces with the clipped eyelids had a slightly frantic look, as if they
wanted at all costs to be different from what
(but what was that?) they were.

'I want something more Japanese,' he
had said finally, and he had noticed himself
how ridiculous it sounded.

'But they are all Japanese girls.'

'Yes I know, I can see that. But I am
looking for something more eh . . . '

'Younger? You want young girl?'

'No . . . no, you don't understand. I
want something more . . . real.

'To him they are all "real",' said De
Goede. 'You won't get anywhere this way.'

He spoke a long sentence in Japanese,
in which Arnold could distinguish only the
word *deska* or something like it, because it

recurred again and again and seemed to indicate some sort of question. Each time the Japanese had replied to this *deska* by something that sounded like *Ach so*, but the expression on his face had not changed once.

'As far as I can see he hasn't a clue,' said Arnold, displaying his friendliest smile.

'In this country you have to have patience, my friend,' was De Goede's reply.

The palaver went on endlessly. A hint of reluctance now appeared on the face of their oriental host.

'I want somebody who is not beautiful,' Arnold tried once more.

'Oh my God,' groaned De Goede, 'have you any fish that isn't fresh?'

A silence fell. The man looked at them impassively, but finally said in a tone as though he cared: 'Maybe in one hour I have girl you like.'

When after that one hour she entered, two things were immediately clear to Arnold Pessers. First, that this was the woman he was looking for, and second, that her appearance aroused a tremendous tension in him.

Her name was Satoko, but he would call her that only on this first occasion. Her face, in an image that had been instantaneous, reminded him of a snowy owl he had once seen during a nocturnal drive through a northern mountain landscape. The bird had been visible from afar as a white, frightening object, and, groping for his camera, he had slowly come to a halt on the deserted road. The white mask, turned sideways on the body, had looked straight at him, burning from two round, yellow eyes, mysterious and hostile—but when he began, as cautiously as possible, to get out of the car, the owl had flown away, no, had risen up into the air. And now it was sitting before him, here in Tokyo, in the guise of a woman. She had a voice that matched her face, somewhere between high and low, a sound different from that of most other women. Her English was rudimentary but the silences between the hesitant words heightened the tension.

He told her he wanted to photograph her by Mount Fuji, preferably in different kimonos, and De Goede discussed with her the where and the how, 'for there are millions of possibilities, assuming the wretched mountain is visible at all. It has its head in the clouds half the time.

It gave him a surprise to hear her speak in Japanese. The timbre of her voice deepened and sometimes, when De Goede said something that seemed to strike her as new or unusual, she lifted her mask slightly and said in a low tone, or half-questioningly, or at any rate on a failing note, something that sounded like *mah* or *meh*, a diphthong that would become so dear to him. Finally, De Goede had reserved a 'real' ryokan for them, in Ukai-Toriyama.

'One or two rooms?'

'I don't know what the custom here is.'

'Usually it's not a question of how to start but how to stop.'

The next day it was radiant autumn weather. She was at the hotel exactly on time.

'Today we can see Fuji.'

It was very early in the morning but the traffic was already under way. They drove along a raised highway below which an unending landscape of drab human activity lay stretched out, but he paid no attention to it. Soon he would be outside the city and see the real Japanese countryside. Something of Hokusei's one hundred views of the sacred mountain would become true, something of the graceful silence from a hundred haikus, of the inimitable, mystical emotion for Basho's journey to the north. It was a good thing that De Goede was not there to read his thoughts.

'There is Fuji-san,' she said suddenly.

He looked but saw nothing. In front of them drove a gigantic tank truck, its stench blowing through the open window.

'I don't see anything,' he said, and a thought flashed through him like a sudden stab of pain: *This woman frightens me.* Taking one hand off the steering wheel she pointed to a spot on the horizon that was as empty as the rest of the sky.

'You must look well.'

Suddenly he saw it. In the emptiness of the still-smog-shrouded sky, there stood, faintly as almost nothing, the outline of the mountain, but in a way that it looked as though the sky was the solid element and the mountain an empty space cut out of it. There was something very ethereal, shadowy, non-existent about it.

'I cannot stop here,' she said apologetically.

He did not reply, and wondered how this day would pass. In the back of the car lay two kimonos, one light and one dark, folded with infinite care. The obis lay beside them, and the one on top, gold-coloured, caught the light of the sun and shone and burnt like fire. He tried to imagine what she would look like in these kimonos, and watched the strong, closed profile beside him. Thinking of the light, he asked how long it would be before they were there.

'There are many places.'

He decided to leave it all to God, and leant back in his seat. Everything he saw filled him with hilarity, not of the merry but of the ecstatic kind. Perhaps one should simply call it a feeling of happiness. He could see how ugly it all was, but the beauty of the ideograms and the script on billboards, road signs and trucks compensated for the larger ugliness, and anyway, they would soon be out of town. Only then would they be in Japan. Through the bends in the road the mountain could sometimes be glimpsed, sometimes not, and in the end it vanished altogether. A man motioned the traffic to leave the second lane but when they came closer Arnold saw it was a robot. The ominous feeling thus created, by the deadly regularity with which the mechanical hand executed its movements, he shrugged off. Later, much later, he would remember that robot as the first herald of a calamity that had something to do both with him and with Japan. Where the two converged, there lay his destiny. That was more or less how it had been.

That day he saw more views of Mount Fuji than Hokusei had ever drawn. Sometimes it looked as if it was all a deception, as if there were thousands of such mountains. They would suddenly reappear, behind a village, a wood, a field, always with that transparent snowy peak that sometimes seemed to float mysteriously in the sky, and then again to rest on solid matter. He could not get a grip on it. From time to time he asked her to stop, ran up a hill, looked at the mountain through trees, or lying in the grass, or across the dark water of a lake in which it was reflected and therefore seemed twice as mysterious, but each time he tried, peering in his viewfinder, to imagine her in the picture, he knew it wasn't right. What he wanted,

not so much for the brochure as for himself,
was a place where the woman and the
mountain would belong together in perfect
counterpoise, would merge into each
other, would hold each other in an unprov-
able but self-evident equilibrium. It should
never be a woman by a mountain, a mountain with a woman in the foreground, or a
woman with a mountain in the background. He himself, the photographer,
would have to be present in it invisibly and
at the same time passionately, and he did
not know how this was to be done. The
mountain, though there was no dear way
of proving it, was an erotic manifestation,
its tall, pointed shape would add something
to the eroticism of her face, as if it had
become the symbol of a breast that had to
exemplify, in the photograph, her breasts,
confined under the kimono; a woman's

breast turned towards the sun, away from the earth, representing, perhaps being, her invisible breasts, and thus floating through the sky, unapproachable, forbidding, and therefore arousing a longing that would become associated with her, though no one seeing the photograph would be able to say why.

7

After they had been driving for some time she said she knew of a place where she had been photographed before, in the same season of the year, for 'Swedish magazines'. The advantage of that place was that she could change her clothes there, and also that it was not far from the ryokan where they would be spending the night. Without waiting for his comment she stopped a few moments later at a tea house by a bend in the road.

Later, when it was all over, he would ponder this question a great deal: when does such a thing as a great love begin? Perhaps it had already begun the first time he saw a portrait of a woman by Utamaro, perhaps during his long flight across the ocean, perhaps when he first saw her at the agency, or perhaps not. A great love, that inexpressible thing, poisoned by banality, probably started with the longing for one. And that longing he had had all his life. That had been the preparation for the moment he was standing here, listening to her voice in the tea house, to the unintelligible ripple of question and answer in which permission was sought and granted, to change, in one of the establishment's other rooms, from her European clothes into one of the kimonos she had brought with her.

She disappeared. He sat down by a window and looked out over a deep valley that, passing all kinds of capricious green-ery, declined into a golf course and then sprang up again, both dark and airy, in the form of woodland, climbing up undulating, compelling slopes, in order to support the mountain that rode through the skies like a god in his chariot.

When she returned he realized just how much he was in love. It was a feeling he remembered from his school days, it raged through his body, it carried within it every possibility of pleasure and grief. The kimono was a rusty, burning colour, a stain of living decay kept in check by the chrysanthemum-golden constraint of the obi. She went out onto the terrace where an imitation temple gate stood waiting for all the world's amateur photographers.

'This very Japanese.'

The white peak of Mount Fuji hung above her head like the crown of the Snow Queen, the mass of the mountain itself draped her shoulders and flowed over the paltry, so very Japanese, gate. He went up to her to measure the light on her face, which had received a rosy glow from the sun.

'Yes, very Japanese,' he said.

So this was the equilibrium. Mountain, woman, gate.

She was a perfect model. Again and again she knew, by means of minute changes of pose and expression, how to devise different pictures for him. He had a phrase for it: she eats the light, and this was possible only because she knew exactly where the light was, her light. She worked with the light, she stole the light, she sculpted herself in ever-different poses so that an eagerness grew in him which, when they finally stopped, made him feel dizzy. He let himself sink down onto the cold grass against one of the pillars of the gate and gazed at the mountain.

'Okay?' she asked.

'Yes. Very good.'

'I change dress?'

'Yes.'

She vanished. Tiny steps of her white feet. A shuffle almost. The kimono's silk made the sound of a large bird flying low overhead.

The evening sky rose from the valley and drifted in veils across the road.

'Where do we go now?'

'Ukai-Toriyama.'

Why had he not remembered it? Ukai-Toriyama. He savoured the sounds, pronounced them softly. This would always remain extraordinary: to sit beside a stranger in a car, on the way to a place you had never heard of. Ukai-Toriyama. The strands of mist danced in the light of the car.

He closed his eyes.

'Here it is,' she said softly.

Whether he had been asleep for a long time or not, he did not know, only that he had dreamt that he was still in the aeroplane high above the ocean, on the way to her.

8

They drove into an avenue flanked by tail torches mounted on poles, burning against the still-pale-coloured evening sky. When he got out of the car he heard the sound of a water wheel and the isolated monotone notes of a string instrument.

'What is that?'

'What you mean?

'This sound. Ting, ting?'

'Oh. This is samisen.'

Samisen, a very light word.

Two servants in black took the suitcase.
The kimonos she wanted to carry herself.
Something restrained him from entering
the low building inside which all contours
were blurred by the faint shine of a lamp.
It was still not altogether dark, he wanted
to walk for a while.

'I will come later.'

She looked at him but said nothing. I
suppose it is un-Japanese, he thought, as he
walked away. Randomly he turned into a
path that led past the outbuildings of the
inn. In the kitchen he saw cooks and girls
in blue aprons. They could not see him.
The path wound through low hills. To his
left he heard the sound of a fast-flowing
stream. He had a feeling as if his soul,
which he must have lost somewhere above
the ocean, was slowly joining him again.

Somewhere in a bend of the path there stood a kind of altar on which several Buddhas were seated. They wore faded red sashes and sat there, detached from everything, against a background of leafless fruit trees behind which loomed a sudden round hill covered with conifers. Now I have arrived, he thought. Now I have truly arrived. Just as in the water where a lighter and a deeper tone could be heard, so a second, more distant hill became visible in the light gap between the dark conifers. He walked on. These Buddhas could never change their expression, the seasons that would cause the leaves of these fruit trees to brighten, fade and drop again had no influence on their faces, they themselves were the seasons. In front of them there were flowers of a furious purple, on the ground lay some thrown-away orange fruit he did not recognize. He bent down, picked one up, pushed the hard skin aside with his thumb and ate from the sweet orange flesh. Then he turned to the purple flowers again. The leaves were long and narrow but the flowers themselves had a crumpled look, drops like quicksilver adhered to the green sepals. There was a curious oneness in everything, the sound of the water, the darkness that slowly fell upon the world, making the mist intenser, more sombre in colour; it all seemed to be one thing. And then there was the sound of the crickets, even now, in October, and that was what they cried, October, October.

He walked towards the sound of the water. From a bare bush between black bamboo stems there hung a single, blackened leaf, not by a stalk but by the broken, floating thread of a spider's web. It was as if nature, the otherness, that which surrounded him, wanted to penetrate him, take possession of him. He shivered and returned to the ryokan. A servant showed him to his cabin and called something.

'Hai!'

The servant motioned him to take off his shoes and slid the door open. She stood as if posing for a photograph, and photographers know best what that means. She wanted to be seen in her chosen stage setting, and then preserved.

Arnold Pessers could never took at a photograph without thinking of this. He found nothing more fascinating than photographs of strangers, taken by strangers, preferably so long ago that all the people concerned were sure to be dead. And sometimes he was absolutely certain that he himself was taking such a photograph, a picture that an anonymous passer-by would one day, somewhere, find on a stall or in a store. What would that stranger see? He would see what Arnold Pessers, the then nameless photographer, saw now, stained by the passage of time—but that could always be cleaned off—a Japanese woman in a kimono, standing in a low, sober room, to her left a kakemono with a single flower painted on it. Other than a low table there was no furniture in the room.

Her kimono was grey with red and gold flames, her piled-up hair gleamed in the same yellowish light that also shone on her intent face. She stood motionless, frozen, stage-managed. With his miniature camera and flash he took her in Ekta-chrome, rapidly and so rhythmically that the soft hissing clicks of the shutter sounded like a metronome.

Something passed, not seconds, but photographic time, a time in which time was swallowed up and preserved.

When he had finished, he said, 'You are very beautiful.' The limitation of this phrase pleased him. Only when people understood few words could they understand everything. This was very comforting, a shared language always spoilt so much, because, he reflected, as soon as words were uttered, lies were spoken.

The door opened. A girl in a simple blue kimono entered on her knees, pushing a small wicker basket containing hot cloths ahead of her across the floor. A second girl brought a dish of raw fish and two rough earthenware sake pitchers, rather like miniature Greek amphorae with only one handle, of the sort that are laid on their sides in the fire. Satoko had sat down with much rustling of her kimono and poured out for him, the snowy mask bending forward, the black gleam of her hair towards him.

'Raw carp. Fish from river. From Ukai.'

Raw carp, starlings, quail, a fish called ayu, tofu, quail's eggs stuck on wooden pins, river trout impaled on spikes in a last undulating motion, everything was pushed into the room, accompanied by the muttering of soft, murmured formulas the servitude of the girls was soundlessly commuted into her own, she grilled, poured, smiled—but if this signified anything or not, he did not know, for she scarcely spoke. So they sat crouched on their zabutons like a Japanese couple after twenty years of married life together. From time to time they looked at each other, indicating with their eyes or with foolish little gestures that this or that was delicious. Whenever his bowl was empty, she refilled it for him. Each of her movements was of a flowing gracefulness, there was nothing left to wish, to desire, to ask. From outside there still came very softly the sound of the samisen, weaving its golden thread through the silence and the almost inaudible purr of the water wheel. After the green, slightly bitter tea, she very briefly and very lightly put her hand on his knee.

'We shall walk garden?'

The torches cast pools of dark, theatrical light on the glistening wet tiles of the garden path. He felt surrounded by sounds, but each of these sounds was small and in itself insignificant, the brook, a waterfall, the slowly churning wheel, the shuffling of her high wooden sandals on the ground, the fronts of her kimono brushing against each other, the sighing of the wind in the bizarre nocturnal shrubs. She had taken his hand, it was as if she was performing a dance with him, a dance in the labyrinth of that garden that could not exist anywhere except in an age gone for ever. Behind the rice-paper windows he saw the shadows of other people, from some of the small houses with pointed thatched roofs there came the sounds of laughter and music. It existed, he thought, and at the same time it did not exist. He did not belong to it, he was here with her and yet he had nothing to do with it. It would cast him out in the same way that a body rejects a transplanted heart. He tried to push aside the word 'dream', but it kept floating to the surface and what he felt was again that crazy mixture of sadness and happiness, so intense that he could hardly bear it. And all the time, persistently he remained the professional photographer, he went on looking, taking pictures with his eyes—a water barrel, a dwarf tree, a chrysanthemum like a weapon, a rustling shadowy crop of reeds.

When they returned to their own little house, the light was muted, and at the place where the table had stood there now lay, on the gently springy rush mats, a bed with a light quilt turned back at one corner.

That night there began the only real love story of his life. When, later, he once tried to talk about it with friends, he discovered that you can speak of such things only in the most basic terms and that these are at the same time the terms that most arouse ridicule and incredulity. But it could not be helped. It was a passion that would burn him down to his roots and through which all that came before and after would fade, because this time it was love first and foremost and only secondly a story. Pleasure, they say, is forgotten as easily as pain, and perhaps this is true. But the event was unforgettable. What he had felt he would have to experience every time afresh in order to know it again, but what he had seen had remained—the shadow dance of torches and bamboo stems outside against the paper screens, the absolute, relentless intensity of everything she did, the mingling of sweat and tears on the white, gleaming face which had remained a mask, then and for ever after, the tension and the bursting into a hundred fragments of her body, which would always haunt his memory, rotating sequences of close-ups, of her matt, translucent skin, the shape of her breasts, of her open, outstretched arms catching him somewhere in the air and pulling him down, and especially the gesture of a hand held desperately in front of her face in order to hide the highest ecstasy while the other fluttered helplessly through the air and then fell like a bird that will never rise again.

Later, when she slept in a forlornness such as he had never seen in anyone, he lay looking at her and wondered what was to happen to him. Three masks she was now wearing, one on top of the other, the Asiatic, that of her own impenetrability, and the third, equally unrevealing veil of sleep. Long ago, on the dresser in his parents' house, there had stood a sculpture of a girl's head. It was, his father had told him, the death mask of an unknown girl who had been drowned in the River Seine. No one knew her name. It was someone who had existed and who now existed no longer, no one would ever know who she had been. That sculpture had frightened him, and fear was what he felt now. He would like to take her photograph but he did not dare. The light of the flickering torches outside fanned across her face as if wishing to awaken her to life again. Gently he covered her round, gleaming shoulders and turned away from her. Something had begun that would obsess him for the rest of his life.

9

For the rest of his life. Five years ago he had first thought that, and it had never changed. He stared blankly at the girl before him who was telling him that the espresso bar was closing. 'We close, we close.' He paid and got up. The five years between that first night and this moment when he was walking through the Ginza like a desolate stranger, he had spent mostly outside Japan, but it seemed like one long curved leap of time in which everything had had to do with her. The morning after that first night they had taken photographs in the neighbourhood, and towards noon they had gone back to the inn at Ukai-Toriyama. He had noticed a strange, sweetish fragrance and asked her what it was.

'It is Mokusei.'

Mokusei is one of the few Japanese plants that smell, he learnt later, and that was what he had called her from then on. Now she had three names, one secret, only known to him as Snowy Mask, her own, Satoko, which he never used, and Mokusei. By that name he wrote to her, it was a name that existed only for them. How easily, he now thought, could the history of those five years be summed up. During that first visit they had stayed together day and night. But she had refused to come to Europe with him.

'My parents, when I go, they die.'

He had never met those parents. They lived in Osaka, and she did not want to take him there. At their parting she had cried and he himself had sat in the plane hunched in his misery. Back in the Netherlands he felt restless, roamed about like a homeless animal, pestered his friends with stones about her, which they found at first amusing and later boring. His relations with women acquired something mechanical, something abstracted, as if it was not really permissible to have anything to do with them, and of course in a way this was so. Finally only those of his women friends remained who were either excited by his total lack of interest or who found it convenient for other reasons which, out of self-preservation, he preferred not to know about. Often, during such encounters, he imagined what she might be doing now, he calculated what time it must be where she was, and it was probably his concealed rage at such thoughts that made the relationship so fascinating for his partner of the moment. After one such meeting he had torn everything from the wall, in seething despair, including her portraits, because he felt she should no longer be a witness to what he regarded as betrayal. On the bare wall above his desk he had hung a Hokusai reproduction. It was the severed head of a woman. The eyes were closed, two lonely dark lines, but the mouth, of which the lower lip was redder than the other, was open. A lizard was sitting on the chin, and the head lay among reeds, amid the loose waves of its own hair. To the right of the face there glimmered a patch of blood, very lightly painted; this red and the green of the lizard were the only living colours, all else was brown; the single, light brush strokes of the reeds had been drawn across the still face. Sometimes it looked as though it were laughing, or trying to say something. He thought it ought not really to hang there, but it wasn't frightening, in spite of the bee which hung almost directly above the face and which, when he was alone and looked for long enough, he could hear buzzing. One of his woman friends had said it was morbid, and he agreed that this was so.

But there was nothing to be done about it. His phone bill soared to astronomic heights and the conversations left a burning emptiness that could be filled only by more conversations. Sometimes she was away from home for days, but he had learnt not to ask questions about that. Her voice was a mask as well, it seemed. He knew nothing about her life. Her parents, her work, that was all. Once he had asked De Goede if he could not find out a bit more about her, but he had said, No, I can't, my friend, that is not what I am for, and he had felt ashamed. She did not want to come to him, De Goede's efforts in that direction, which he had undertaken without objection, had been of no avail. After a time, his friend had been transferred to Singapore, and so the last person they both knew had gone.

During his leave in Brussels they had dined together and De Goede had advised him to break it off. 'Believe me, I have seen it before, you must end it or you'll go to pieces yourself.' Arnold had got drunk and asked why his friend always wore such ridiculous pocket handkerchiefs, and De Goede had replied 'for fear of death', and then they had got drunk together nd misbehaved themselves in a Japanese restaurant, and that was not the only time that Arnold Pessers got drunk in a Japanese restaurant.

But whenever he obtained a commission that enabled him to travel to Japan, she was at the airport, and they went back to her Tokyo flat as if he had never been away. He always tried to stay as long as possible, on one occasion for almost six months. That his debts in the Netherlands mounted, and his bank would no longer give him credit, worried him more than he admitted to himself but because of the distance it seemed as if these things could not be quite real, and anyway, his whole existence had become unreal, as if all this were not happening to him but to a stranger, a hired actor who, when he looked in the mirror, bore a curious resemblance to him, Arnold Pessers. Sometimes she left for a few days.

Then he stayed alone in her flat and went into the city in the evenings and sat among the other expatriate Europeans in the Pub Cardinal in Roppongi or hung around in discos where Japanese disguised as Negroes in raffia shorts served the drinks, or where electric miniature trams whirred all along the wails, until he had reached the right pitch of insanity. This was definitely the 'other' Japan, a spiritual slum of failed imitations, a country he hated the way you hate a rival. All those things that he loved her for, the remoteness, the enigma, the inaccessibility, here seemed to have been converted into their opposites, showing him a different mask, of mechanized vulgarity, that threatened him and would eventually drive him away. But he never spoke of this to her.

10

That was how it had been until now, until this strange, silent moment, when he was walking here and heard his own footsteps on the emptying pavement. But this evening everything had become different. The sword, he reflected, that he had so long expected had struck, flashing, deadly.

She had taken him out to dinner at the Imperial Hotel, and in that sumptuous setting she had told him that this was the last time he would see her, because she was going to be married. It had sounded like a lesson learnt by rote. 'I want to be near parents. I don't want to make trouble. I want to make house and have children.' The fact that she had added I love you, with that slight hesitation in the l that had always attracted him so, was no help. He had told her for the hundredth time that he too wanted to be married and have children, but then her face closed again, showing that it was impossible.

'It cannot be.'

He had come to the end of his thoughts, to the end of his walk, and entered the flat. She slept her dead, drowned sleep, but this time he would take her photograph. From his suitcase, which was already packed because they were going to Ukai-Toriyama the next day, also for the last time, he took his tripod and an ultrafast film. He would have to use a flash. He rearranged the sheet a little. If it was too smooth she would look really dead in the photograph. That was superstition of course—probably because that 'dead' look was part of her sleep, but in the photograph he wanted to be able to see by the colour and the details surrounding her that she was really *asleep*. Someone who is asleep is at the same time nearby and far away, from you and from themselves, powerless and yet powerful, precisely because of that distance. Only at the sixth or seventh flash did she wake up.

'I don't like. When I sleep it is not me.'

'Yes, it is you. I know.'

'No. When I sleep I have no eyes. I am not blind person.'

She turned over. He lay down beside her, but he did not fall asleep until it was almost morning. He felt the warmth of that body of which he knew every tiny detail and which he had seen in an ecstasy he would never again—he was certain of this—be able or want to arouse in anyone. And at the same time he realized that he knew nothing about her and never would. He would have liked to break her open in order to know her secret or at least to find out what her feelings for him were, if she had any. He fell into his sleep as if into a fathomless hole in which he would have preferred to remain. But farewells had to be said first.

11

That last day became a replica of the first. The time between these two days, with all those longings, letters, declarations, nights of love, all those dramatic phone calls across the grey steppes of Siberia, evaporated and were annihilated in the one moment that, with the eternal mountain still floating in the distance, he took the picture he had already taken five years earlier. Even in the prints, later, you could not see that the woman standing there had grown five years older, still less the sacred mountain. The same woman, the same photograph, the same autumn day, the same inn, the same smell of Mokusei. Life as memory: the samisen, the water wheel, the torches, the servant preceding them. This time again, as before, he wanted to go out for a walk. With a movement of her hand she checked him. She pulled him down beside her on the tatami, undressed him, undressed herself. Never before had she been the one to take the initiative. They lay naked on the mat beside the low table. This, he thought, is war rather than anything else. Fury mingled with her love, a fury that corresponded to his own. Biting, devouring, penetrating the other, absorbing, robbing, with all the hopeless frenzy of people who want to become each other, want to be one but cannot, who are always again forced to part, to leave each other, gathering empty rooms behind themselves in which gestures and words, the maimed language of never-finished phrases, will dissolve among the impassive objects waiting for the next guests or not waiting but merely existing. He felt like someone who has to swim an immense distance and has come halfway, too far to go back and too far to go on. When she finally let go, turned over, away from him, burying her face in the fine rushes of the tatami, when her whole body had once again become a closed, unassailable fortress, an object he had no longer anything to do with, he stood up, dressed and went outside. It was a shade darker than the first time. He walked past the Buddhas. Here, too, nothing had changed; with difficulty they had counted out one second in those five years. A dwarfish old woman, bent low under a heavy burden of brushwood, came towards him like a bad omen. Branches, fire, ashes. The brook rippled, and who should he have been, to hear a sound different from that of the first time? He walked further than on that other occasion. On the wet path he saw the furry skin of a nut, trampled, crushed. All objects now seemed to acquire a meaning, the discolorations in the last green that could still be discerned, the fungi on a tree, black, damp patches on the bark of a birch, every thing was trying to say something. From time to time he paused, registering the movement of the swift water past a gleaming black boulder. It was as if he was counting something, but he did not know what it might be. Even if he could have done so, he would not now have wished to take any photographs—this, for once, would not be preserved, this was for him, and only for him. He took a path leading upwards, into the darkness, stepping on some thick, smooth bamboo canes that had been placed across the stream as a footbridge, listened to the gurgling and swallowing of the water. What vanished feet had worn away this path, had made it into nature? Under the surface of the water the ground itself seemed to be aflow. Somewhere there lay a pile of logs, a firm dark shape as if they had grown together. A hundred years ago a woodcutter had been here, had stacked them ready for the next day but had never come back. Mokusei. He heard himself saying her name aloud, and he stood still. So this was fear, what he was now feeling. Something irreparable was happening to him. He turned around. Out of the direction from which he had come, strands of mists moved towards him, shredded, floating shapes intent on attacking him, ready to encircle him, envelop him, hold him imprisoned by that stack of wood, a hundred years, a thousand years, for ever.

When, panting and scratched and still pursued by the mists, he arrived, running and stumbling, at the inn, her car was no longer there. The faces of the servants expressed nothing. He went to their room and slid back the door. On the table there was only one rice bowl. For the second time that evening he heard himself saying her name while she was not there. Mokusei. He took off his shoes, went in and crouched by the table. Now he had to enter upon the sadness that would never leave him all his life, even if he lived for a long time. It would fade, like everything else, but he would never escape the feeling that it was he himself that was fading away.

Aiku-Wakamatsu, Amsterdam
Autumn 1980